Dedicated to my parents and grandparents, who surrounded my childhood
with nature and filled it with memories that will never fade.
—E.S.

For Iz and her boundless imagination.
—D.O.

ISBN 978-1-4671-9714-4

Published by Arcadia Children's Books
A division of Arcadia Publishing, Inc.
Charleston, South Carolina
www.arcadiapublishing.com

Visit Shankman & O'Neill at www.shankmanoneill.com

Printed in China

10 9 8 7 6 5 4 3 2 1

the LAKE I ♥ LOVE

BY ED SHANKMAN   PICTURES BY DAVE O'NEILL

arcadia®
CHILDREN'S BOOKS

Shankman and O'Neill
children's books

There's a lake that I know in the middle of nowhere,
And when I was little, we all used to go there.
The calm water lapped at the shore like a kiss,
And I've found that's a sound I have since come to miss.

At the edge of the lake was a thin strand of sand,
Where my parents and I used to stroll, hand in hand,
As the bugs and the birds formed a musical band
Whose songs, I was sure, were the best in the land.

There were times that I'd roll in the sand on my back,
And I have to admit that I had quite a knack.
Yes, I wiggled in ways some did not understand,
But I left some *spectacular* shapes in the sand!

Then I'd play with a stick or a shovel and pail,
Building castles like those in an old fairy tale.

Or a boat with a sail
made for chasing a whale,

Or at least a small home
for a frog or a snail.

Or I might dip my ten
tiny toes in the lake,

Which, on cold afternoons,
may have been a mistake.

But on days that were just
a bit warmer than that,

I'd go all the way in
with a jump and a *splat!*

Then I'd swim like a fish or a duck or an eel
Or a frog or a tadpole or maybe a seal.
(Now to swim like a seal has a special appeal—
It's a thrill you can feel from your head to your heel!)

Just picture the fishes that called that lake home—
That would wriggle and dive, blow their bubbles, and roam.
There were catfish and minnows and sunfish and trout.
Every fish you could wish for was swishing about!

Not to mention the creatures who lived *near* the water—
A bunny, a chipmunk, a toad and his daughter,
A snake and some squirrels, a mouse and a fox,
And a few sleepy turtles that lay on the rocks.

There were beetles and butterflies, spiders, and bees,
Ladybugs, katydids, inchworms, and fleas,
Centipedes, dragonflies, darners, and ants,
And one yellow jacket *without* matching pants.

(yellow pants?)

It was just like a movie or some picture book
To see all these creatures wherever we'd look.
They ran and they sat and they ate and they hid;
They did all the same things that the rest of us did.

It was so nice to see them all happy and free.
And I wondered if they thought the same about me.

And, of course, there were flowers all over the place.
There were buttercups, daisies, and old Queen Anne's lace.
My grandmother seemed to know each flower's face,
And she taught me to cherish their beauty and grace.

The lake was surrounded by acres of trees,
With thousands of leaves that would dance in the breeze.
We could pass a whole day in those woodlands with ease,
And hear no other sound but the birds and the bees.

My grandpa would say, "It's so peaceful and quiet."
And I would repeat the same phrase just to try it.
It felt so appealing, that "so peaceful" feeling,
That stretched from the ground to the tall leafy ceiling.

The sun dappled down through the leaves all around,
Splashing light on the tree trunks and light on the ground.
And those splashes of light were so happily bright,
That the sight of them filled both our hearts with delight.

Yes a kingdom of trees, ripe for hanging or climbing,
Or sometimes just sitting and silently rhyming.
With creatures above me and others below,
(There were creatures with features that I didn't know)!

My friend and I played in that forest for hours.
The twigs were our swords and the trees were our towers.
We wandered and watched. We talked and explored.
Then we gathered some sticks that we carefully stored.

We built all kinds of hideouts. And that's where we hid—
From a ghost or a goblin, a mom, or a kid.
Who cared if a martian or wolf was behind us.
We weren't afraid because *no one could find us!*

We never ran out of new ways to have fun.
Or new places to climb or to roll or to run.
If we had to invent a new game, then we would.
Sometimes making it up was what made it so good!

For example, we might solve some kind of a mystery,
That hadn't been solved throughout all human history.

That's only, of course, if we weren't too busy, spinning in circles to make ourselves dizzy.

We would play in this way
till the end of the day,
Then we'd watch as the light
gently faded away.

It turns out fading light
puts on quite a display!
We could not look away
till the very last ray.

It wasn't long after the sunlight would fade,
That the crickets eased into their sweet serenade.
As we silently followed the sounds that they made,
I thought no finer rhythms had ever been played.

Think of tiny maracas and small castanets.
That's a combo that nobody ever regrets.
I heard washboards and rhythm sticks, wood blocks and rattles,
And tapping on cymbals with very soft paddles.

The beat was just so, when the volume would grow,
And the fireflies added some light to the show.
(For those who want magic but can't seem to find it,
Try firefly light with some crickets behind it.)

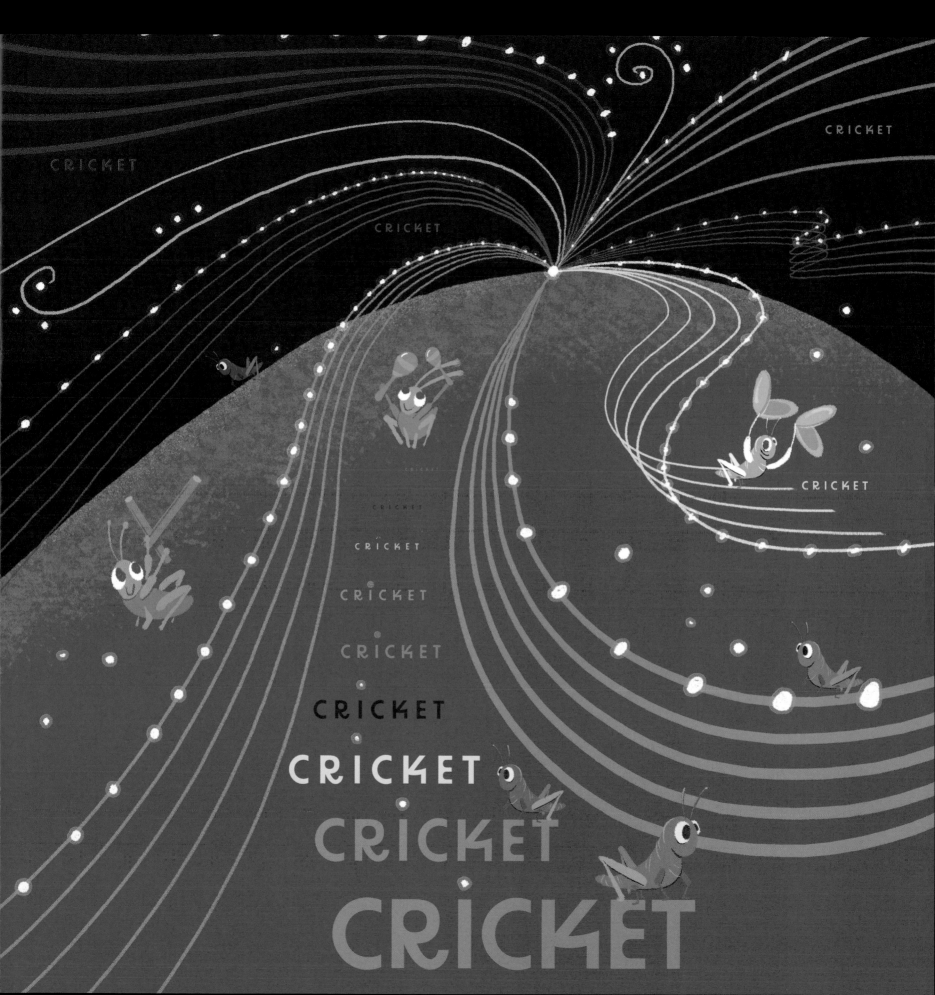

Well, all of that buzzing and flashing and humming,
Meant evening was here and our dinner was coming!

Maybe the grownups would grill up a steak,
And we'd eat it outside by the side of the lake.
Now there's something about eating out with the birds,
That makes a kid want to take seconds and thirds.

(It did seem like I ate a *lot* in that place.
Of course, most of the food ended up on my face.
But I never did mind when my food left a trace,
Because if I was starved, it was there just in case!)

We slept in a bungalow,
cozy and small,
That somehow had just
enough space for us all.
My parents would tuck us
both into our beds
With a few loving words
and a kiss on our heads.

For just a few minutes,
I'd lie there awake,
And I'd let my thoughts drift
with the sound of the lake.
Till the moon's silver beams
turned my thoughts into dreams.
And a bedtime like that's
just as nice as it seems.

It was quite late one
evening in June or July,
That my dad woke me up to
come look at the sky.
The stars were so clear
and so big and so near,
That I felt I could reach out
and touch them *right here!*

And the feeling I got
looking up from that spot,
Was a sense of pure magic
I never forgot.
It was there in the air,
in the cool summer breeze—
In that soft lapping water
surrounded by trees . . .

. . . in the sound of the crickets,
the scent of the flowers,
The shadowy night that
would stay dark for hours.

Later my mom tucked me back in my bed,
But all of that magic was still in my head.
I knew in the morning, I'd wake up and see
That magical world out there waiting for me.

Of course, that was a long time ago, it is true.
I've seen more lakes since then and some other things, too.

I've seen far away cities and oceans and streams.
I've had great adventures and followed my dreams.

Yes, I've traveled the world like a wandering dove,
But I'll always come back to the lake that I love.

Also by Ed Shankman and Dave O'Neill

The Boston Balloonies

The Bourbon Street Band Is Back

Camp and Me By the Maple Tree

The Cods of Cape Cod

I Met a Moose in Maine One Day

Maddie and Liam at the Museum

Monkey See, Zebra Do

My Grandma Lives in Florida

The Sea Lion's Friend

When a Lobster Buys a Bathrobe

Where's the Bathroom?

A Whimsical Washington Night

Also by Ed Shankman, with Dave Frank

I Went to the Party in Kalamazoo

Ed Shankman's entire life has been one long creative project. He has been writing children's books since he himself was a child. He performed for many years as a lead guitar player, and is an impassioned, if imperfect, painter. He has also published his novel, *The Backstage Man*, which was written over the course of three decades. And he spent his professional career directing creative teams within the advertising industry. He lives with his wife, Miriam, who is the love of his life.

Dave O'Neill is an Illustrator and Art Director. Throughout his career, Dave has worked with several advertising and marketing agencies where he specialized in children's brands and event planning but he'd rather be drawing animals wearing hats. When he's not bringing Ed's rhymes to life, he lends his design skills to The Growing Stage—The Children's Theatre of New Jersey. Dave and Ed have created twelve additional books in the Shankman & O'Neill library and believe a movie studio should approach them with plans for a cinematic MOOSE-iverse. Today, Dave is a husband to a cool, talented girl and a father to a cool, talented, smaller girl. More of Dave's work can be found on his art blog, at oneilldave.blogspot.com.

children's boo

www.shankmanoneill.co